D0368465

DISCARD

Fishing Queen

by Marci Peschke
illustrated by Tuesday Mourning

PICTURE WINDOW BOOKS
a capstone imprint

Kylie Jean is published by Picture Window Books
A Capstone Imprint
1710 Roe Crest Drive
North Mankato, Minnesota 56003
www.mycapstone.com

Copyright © 2018 by Picture Window Books

All rights reserved. No part of this publication may be reproduced in whole or in part, or stored in a retrieval system, or transmitted in any form or by any means, electronic, mechanical, photocopying, recording, or otherwise, without written permission of the publisher.

Library of Congress Cataloging-in-Publication Data
Cataloging-in-Publication information is on file with the Library of Congress.
Names: Peschke, Marci, author. | Mourning, Tuesday, illustrator.
Title: Fishing Queen
ISBN 978-1-4795-9900-4 (library binding)
ISBN 978-1-4795-9902-8 (paper over board)
ISBN 978-1-4795-9906-6 (eBook PDF)

Creative Director: Nathan Gassman
Graphic Designer: Sarah Bennett
Editor: Shelly Lyons
Production Specialist: Laura Manthe.

Design Element Credit:
Shutterstock: blue67design, Marina Mandarina

Printed and bound in the United States of America.
010368F17

For Maggie and her grandpa who loved
to fish! With love from Mimi
— MP

Table of Contents

All About Me, Kylie Jean!

My name is Kylie Jean Carter. I live in a big, sunny, yellow house on Peachtree Lane in Jacksonville, Texas, with Momma, Daddy, and my two brothers, T.J. and Ugly Brother.

T.J. is my older brother, and Ugly Brother is . . . well . . . he's really a dog. Don't you go telling him he is a dog. Okay? I mean it. He thinks he is a real true person.

He is a black-and-white bulldog. His front looks like his back, all smashed in. His face is all droopy like he's sad, but he's not.

His two front teeth stick out, and his tongue hangs down. (Now you know why his name is Ugly Brother.)

Everyone I love to the moon and back lives in Jacksonville. Nanny, Pa, Granny, Pappy, my aunts, my uncles, and my cousins all live here. I'm extra lucky, because I can see all of them any time I want to!

My momma says I'm pretty. She says I have eyes as blue as the summer sky and a smile as sweet as an angel. (Momma says pretty is as pretty does. That means being nice to the old folks, taking care of little animals, and respecting my momma and daddy.)

But I'm pretty on the outside and on the inside. My hair is long, brown, and curly.

I wear it in a ponytail sometimes, but my absolute most favorite is when Momma pulls it back in a princess style on special days.

I just gave you a little hint about my big dream. Ever since I was a bitty baby I have wanted to be an honest-to-goodness beauty queen. I even know the wave. It's side to side, nice and slow, with a dazzling smile. I practice all the time, because everybody knows beauty queens need to have a perfect wave.

I'm Kylie Jean, and I'm going to be a beauty queen. Just you wait and see!

Chapter One

Catfish King

This morning when I wake up, I see that Jack Frost has visited. All of my next-door neighbor, Miss Clarabelle's, flower beds are dusted with a white, icy glaze. Ugly Brother looks out the window with me. He really wants to go to church with us!

"You need to stay here, silly doggy!" I tell him.

"Ruff," he replies. One ruff means no. Two ruffs mean yes.

"Now, go lie down. Maybe I'll bring you a treat," I tell him.

"Ruff, ruff!" he barks. Then he turns around and heads for his doggy bed.

The frost glitters like diamonds as Momma, Daddy, T.J., and I head out to church. Mr. Weatherman had told us we would get some winter weather, and he was right! Because of the cold air, I get to wear my very favorite coat. It's a deep, dusty-rose pink with white fur trim around the hood. But even with my warm coat on, I am puffing out little clouds of air as I breathe.

After church, our whole family heads over to the Catfish King restaurant. Usually we go to Nanny and Pa's Lickskillet Farm for Sunday dinner. But because our family is so big, only some of us can eat inside. The rest have to eat outside. Nobody wants to sit outside today in this freezing weather!

Inside the Catfish King, we have to wait because we are a very large party, and Sunday is one of the busiest days. But I don't mind. The air is warm and rich with the smell of delicious fried catfish. Our whole family is piled into the corner of the waiting area, sitting on benches and chatting.

T.J. says, "Lil' Bit, give me your coat, and I'll go hang it up."

I look at T.J., but I don't hand him my coat. I want to keep it on. It's my favorite dress coat!

"I think I'll keep this on," I tell him.

"Give T.J. your coat, please. We don't eat with our coats on," says Momma.

T.J. holds out his hand. I slowly take off my coat and give it to him. He walks over and hangs up the coats and then sits by our cousin Lilly. T.J. and Lilly are talking about what they're going to order.

Lilly says, "I want tartar sauce with mine!"

"Tartar sauce ruins a piece of tasty catfish," says T.J. "In fact, the best way to eat catfish is plain."

They move on to talking about the homework they have to do for school tomorrow. Meanwhile, I stand by Lilly's younger sister, Lucy. My cousin Lucy and I walk over to look at the community bulletin board by the door. Some people have posted signs on it, looking for lost pets and items.

There are also flyers advertising things for sale and sharing local events.

I see a flyer for the upcoming holiday parade. It's only the beginning of December, so the parade is still almost four weeks away. Below that flyer is another one that catches my eye.

"Hey, look at that flyer with a giant blue cat on it," I say.

Now, I'm not talking about the kind of cat that has four legs and says meow. I mean the swimming kind with long Granddaddy Whiskers that likes to tuck into the mud of a riverbed! It's a catfish!

"It's a fishing contest," I say. "Winter is the best time to catch big blue cats in Texas!"

Lucy reads, "The Winter Catfish Classic Team Fishing Contest will be held on Arrowhead Lake in two weeks. The team with the catch that weighs the most, wins. The prize is a brand new boat and a chance to meet Rick Allen."

Rick Allen is a famous fishing celebrity. Everyone knows all about him. He even has his own show on TV.

T.J.'s ears perk up, and he stops talking with Lilly. He walks over and looks at the sign. "I'm going to enter that contest and win," he says. "Dad, you can be on my team!"

Daddy walks over and says, "I'm in. Sounds like a good time, son!"

Now my ears perk up, because I was thinking of entering the contest too! I lean close to Lucy. "I really want to enter the contest," I whisper. "But T.J. just asked Daddy."

"Maybe you could ask my daddy instead?" Lucy suggests. "You could be a fishing queen!"

I nod my head. "Maybe," I say. "But there might be someone else I can ask."

Just then, the hostess calls our party. As we head on over to our table, I can't help thinking how exciting this fishing contest is! But until I can get some advice from a master fisherman, I'm going to keep my entry a big ol' secret. Fishing Queen has a nice ring to it . . . and you know how I love to be a queen!

Fishing Tip #1

Some catfish can sting! Make sure an experienced adult fisherman or fisherwoman handles a catfish.

Chapter Two
Pond Fishing

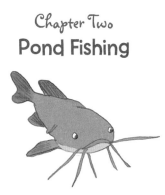

On Monday, when I get home after school,
Momma has a snack ready for me in the kitchen.

"Could this be a to-go snack?" I ask.

"I guess so," Momma replies. "What are you up
to now?"

"I really need to go to Nanny and Pa's farm,"
I tell her.

Momma says, "Why can't it wait until the
weekend, sugar?"

"Could I tell you in the car on the way?" I reply. "It gets dark awfully early now, and I need to visit Pa today."

Momma agrees. I am all ready to go. I am wearing my warmest pink down jacket. Y'all know pink is my favorite color! We head out to the van.

"What is it you need to talk to Pa about?" Momma asks as we drive.

"I have a secret that I need to discuss with him," I tell her.

Momma asks, "Is he helping you build something for a project?"

"No, ma'am," I say.

"Did he ask you to help him with the ducks?" she asks.

"No, ma'am," I say. "You'll just have to wait and see!"

Momma pulls up to Nanny and Pa's. She waves to Nanny as we get out of the van. I head toward the shed next to the barn, and Momma waits.

Inside the shed, I have my own fishing pole, tackle box, fishing vest, and hat. I find it quickly and then walk back out by Momma.

When Momma sees me, she asks, "Is your secret a fishing date with Pa?"

I wink at her. "Yes!" I say. "He just doesn't know it yet!"

Momma laughs as we walk toward the house. Inside, the kitchen is warm and cozy, like being tucked into a quilt. Pa and Nanny give Momma and me big ol' squeezy hugs.

"This is a wonderful surprise!" Nanny says.

"I came to go fishing down at the pond with Pa," I tell her.

Pa grins from ear to ear. He says, "Aren't you something, coming by to do some winter fishing with your ol' Pa."

"It's still pretty cold out there," says Nanny.

"I have my long johns in my backpack," I tell her. "I can wear them under my jeans."

"Well, darlin', you're almost all ready," says Pa. "You put those long johns on, and I'll go get ready. It will just take me a minute."

Pa leaves the kitchen to go find his fishing gear. I leave to go put on my long johns.

When I come back, Nanny has poured two cups of coffee — one for her and one for Momma. They are going to have a little chat while we fish. Pa and I are going to have a little chat too! Pa just doesn't know it yet.

Nanny gives me a thermos of hot chocolate to take to the pond. When Pa comes out, I head for the door.

Momma says, "You two better hurry, or you'll be doing some night fishing instead. It's getting dark pretty early."

Pa and I wave goodbye.

"Don't worry! We'll be back soon," I reply.

Then we grab my fishing gear from the barn and walk side by side to the pond. The late afternoon sun shines on our backs, casting a shadow up ahead.

By the pond, we sit on the dock. Pa has some chicken livers for bait. Some people say catfish like stinky or live bait. Pa pops the top on the tub of livers. Instantly my nose wrinkles up as the smell hits me square in the face.

"Those livers are stink-yyy!" I squeal.

Pa says, "They are several days old and perfect for catching cats!"

We carefully bait our hooks. The pond is stocked with catfish. They are usually easy to catch, especially with the right bait.

Pa and I both toss our lines into the murky water. In no time at all, we each have a catfish on the line! Pa and I reel in our fish. They both make a splish-splash as we toss them into our bucket.

Pa seems to know I'm not just here to fish. He asks, "Are you going to tell me what's on your mind, Kylie Jean?"

"There's going to be a fishing contest on Arrowhead Lake," I tell him. "Have you heard about it? T.J. and Daddy are entering it. Really, I think it's for kids, so you have to have a team.

A team with a kid and a grown-up. I think I could win it, but I need a grown-up."

Pa listens to me intently, but he's quiet.

"I've been fishing on this very pond since I was knee-high to a grasshopper!" I continue. "You're an old fisherman with lots of experience, Pa. You'd be perfect for my team."

Pa laughs. "If you're sure you want to compete against your dad and your brother," he says, "I'll be on your team."

"I'm sure," I reply. "Thank you, Pa!"

Pa nods and smiles. He and I look at the sky, dusty gray and streaked with pale pink stripes. A few stars have started to poke through.

"It's getting dark," I say as I reel in my line.

Pa reels in his line too. Then he takes one side of the handle on the old tin bucket, and I take the other. Together we walk back up to the farmhouse glowing on the hill.

Pa and I drop off our gear in the barn and walk to the house. As we step through the door into the kitchen, Nanny looks into our fish bucket. "Two fish are just right for dinner," she says to Pa. "One for me and one for you!"

"Guess what, Nanny?" I say.

Nanny looks curious. "What, Kylie Jean?"

Pa grins. "We have some big news."

Momma looks at me with suspicious eyes.

"Pa and I are entering the Winter Catfish Classic Team Fishing Contest!" I announce.

"How exciting!" Nanny says. "If we had four fish, you and your momma could stay for dinner to celebrate your news."

"No, ma'am," I say. "It's a school night, and Momma and I have to get home for dinner. But I'm sure we'll be catching a lot of fish for you to cook, since we're going to be fishing all the time to get ready for the contest. I really want to be a fishing queen!"

Fishing Tip #2

The kind of water can affect what color a catfish appears to be. Even the same species can look very different, depending on the water. Blue cats, especially, will appear darker in shallow water and lighter in deep, muddy water. Sometimes they look white in cold, muddy water.

Chapter Three
Fish Food

On Tuesday when I get home from school, the phone rings. Ring . . . ring . . .

I pick it up and say, "Hello?"

Pa says, "Hello. Is this Kylie Jean?"

"Yes, sir, it is," I reply.

He continues, "I have a plan for the fishing contest. I think we should try out some different kinds of bait to see what the fish are biting these days."

"I just love that idea!" I gush.

Pa goes on, "We can use all the help we can get if we want to beat T.J. and your daddy. Can you do a little research at the library to see what the experts suggest?"

"Yes, sir!" I say. "I love the library. The librarian, Ms. Patrick, is one of my very best friends!"

"Sometimes new bait floating down into the murky water is like candy to a catfish," Pa adds. "We always fish with night crawlers, chicken livers, or small fish. I figured special bait might be our secret weapon. You keep me posted. Bye for now."

"I will!" I tell him. "Love you! Bye, Pa."

After I hang up with Pa, I call Lucy. I need someone to help me do my fishing bait research.

"Hello?" Lucy says.

"Hi, Lucy! It's Kylie Jean," I say. "I need an assistant for a special library project. Can you meet me at the library?"

"Sure!" Lucy says. "What are we looking for?"

"Pa and I are entering the fishing contest, and we need to figure out what bait to use. I think we can find some information at the library."

"I don't think that will be too hard to find," she replies. "We can always ask the librarian for help too."

"Great!" I say. "See you soon!"

Momma walks with me to the library. When we arrive, she goes to the magazine area to read. Lucy isn't there yet, so I wait inside the library doors for her. Soon I see Lilly pull up. When the car stops, Lucy jumps out and dashes up the library steps. We go straight to the big library desk.

"Hello, Ms. Patrick," we say.

"Hello, girls," the librarian replies. "How can I help you?"

"Well, I'm entering a fishing contest soon, and I would like to know what kinds of bait catfish like best," I tell her.

Ms. Patrick says, "First, I think you should check the computer catalog to see what books we already have. Don't forget we can check our online databases too."

"Thank you very much, ma'am," I say.

Lucy and I walk over to the computer catalog. I type in "catfish bait" and wait to see what comes up. The catalog suggests *The Secrets of Catfishing*; *Catfishing: A Guide to Catching the Big Fish*; *Catfish*; and *The Complete Catfish*.

I write down the numbers of the books we are looking for. Lucy says, "The library has more catfish books, but they are all checked out!"

"I don't mind," I tell her. "Four is one of my lucky numbers, and I am taking home four books."

Lucy is really good with computers. The encyclopedia database has a lot of information on catfish, and she prints it all out. Now we have a whole stack of fishy facts. We gather our things and find Momma. Then we make our way to the door to wait for Lilly to pick up Lucy.

"Lucy, we should go fishing together tomorrow and try out our new bait ideas!" I say.

"You know, fishing is not my favorite thing," Lucy replies. "Will you put the bait on the hook and take the fish off for me?"

"I'll put the bait on," I say, "and I reckon Pa will take the fish off for you."

"Okay then!" Lucy agrees. "My ride is here. See you tomorrow."

"You're the best cousin in the whole wide world!" I reply. "Thank you for helping me. See you tomorrow!"

* * *

That night, Ugly Brother and I lie on the floor of my bedroom with my library books spread all around us. We pore over the pages of the books, and I take notes. Ugly Brother places a paw on a page. A big ol' bull doggie brother can be a good bookmark!

"You'll never guess what!" I say. "One of these books is written by the famous fishing celebrity Rick Allen!"

Ugly Brother barks, "Ruff, ruff." And that means yes.

At first, I read a lot of things I already know
about catfish. The books say most catfish are
bottom-feeders, which means they swim along the
bottom of the lake with their mouths open and eat
anything in their path. I knew that one already.

I look over at Ugly Brother. "I think you're a bottom-feeder too," I joke. "You're always waiting under the kitchen table with your mouth open!"

But I also read about some shocking choices for bait: Ivory soap, bubble gum, aluminum foil with vanilla on it, and Spam!

Just then, T.J. knocks on my door. He wants to know what I am up to. I put a finger to my lips, looking at Ugly Brother.

"Shhhhh!" I whisper and slide the books out of sight. I stay quiet until T.J. thinks I'm not in my room.

After T.J. leaves, we call Pa.

"Did you read about different kinds of bait?" Pa asks.

"Yup, I found lots of ideas," I tell him.

"Wonderful!" Pa says.

"Oh, I also asked Lucy to tag along with us tomorrow," I add.

"That sounds great. I'll pick you up after school. We can try out the mystery bait at Arrowhead Lake," Pa says.

That night I'm so excited, I can barely sleep. I dream of giant blue cats that smell like vanilla.

Fishing Tip #3

You can fish for catfish day or night.

Chapter Four
Catfish Bait Magic

On Wednesday morning, I get up early to gather bait. Momma helps me find aluminum foil and vanilla, Ivory soap, bubble gum, and Spam. I load them into my backpack and head out to the bus. On the bus, I tell my favorite bus driver, Mr. Jim, that I will not be riding that afternoon. Pa will be picking me up! Lucy does the same. We talk about fishing at recess and lunch. Both of us wonder which bait will work best!

After school, Pa meets us in the parent pickup lane on the side of the school. Lucy and I scoot into his pickup truck and buckle our seat belts.

On the way to a new spot at Arrowhead Lake, we stop at the Sports Shack to sign up for the fishing contest. The sporting goods store actually looks like a shack. It's built out of wood, and inside it smells like fish bait.

Behind a big wooden counter stands Ray, the store owner. He is wearing a fishing vest.

"I'm here to enter the Winter Catfish Classic Team Fishing Contest!" I announce proudly.

"Kids have to be younger than eighteen to enter," Ray says. "And they must have an adult on their team."

"I'm younger than eighteen," I tell him. "And Pa's my grown-up!"

Ray says, "Righty-o, little lady. Just fill out this form, and have your pa sign it at the bottom then."

Good thing I brought my favorite lucky pink ink pen! I show Lucy.

She gives me a thumbs-up and says, "That pen should bring you luck!"

"I sure hope so!" I reply.

Pa and I finish our papers and give them back to Ray. He smiles and gives us a thumbs-up too.

We don't waste any more time at Sports Shack. We hop back in Pa's truck and zoom toward the lake to try out the new bait.

Right before we get to the lake, Pa suggests that we stop for a snack. He pulls into Rayburn's gas station. Pa always likes to get a water and candy to take to the fishing spot.

Lucy and I try to hurry and pick our candy quickly, but there are so many choices! We finally manage to choose a candy bar and grab a bottle of water each. We all pile back into Pa's truck, and soon we arrive at our favorite Lake Arrowhead fishing spot, where we all put on our gear.

"I have some special snacks for the fish!" I
announce.

"Boy, those library books really helped you find
the right snacks!" says Lucy.

"They sure did!" I tell her.

Pa is shocked as I pull out Ivory soap, bubble
gum, aluminum foil with vanilla flavoring on it,
and Spam.

"Bubble gum for fish bait is just crazy," Pa says. "And, Kylie Jean, would you want to eat aluminum foil or soap? I have to say, I don't think so, and the fish won't want it either!"

"These are the bait choices that came up in our research," I tell him. "Let's just give them a try."

"Just because we wouldn't like these things, doesn't mean the fish won't!" Lucy adds.

Pa shrugs his shoulders, "I guess giving them a try can't hurt," he says.

We start with the vanilla aluminum foil.

"Let me bait my own hook," Lucy says. "I can do this one! It doesn't wiggle or stink."

Together, Lucy, Pa, and I sit on the curve of the shoreline under a canopy of tall, green pines.

We all drop a line in the lake, and then we wait. Nothing happens.

Next, we try the soap. Again . . . nothing!

"Sure enough," Pa says, "these fish don't seem to like foil or soap."

Then we try the bubble gum.

"I'd like the bubble gum bait best if I were a fish," I say.

Lucy laughs. "Of course you would. Because pink is your favorite color!" she replies.

After sitting and waiting with the bubble gum on our lines, we still haven't gotten a single blue cat to nibble. Now we only have the Spam left. I bait the hook and cross my fingers behind my back.

"Come on, blue cats!" I plead. And just like that, my bobber dips and disappears!

I feel the tug of the fish, and with a yank of the line, I hook it. I reel it in slowly, and Pa helps me net it.

"One catch doesn't prove a thing, though," he says. "Let's all try the Spam."

Lucy, Pa, and I bait up with Spam, and we all catch fish! Over and over, we catch fish with Spam bait.

By now, the sun is sinking lower and lower in the evening sky.

"Before you know it, the sky will be as dark as the inside of a deep pocket," I say.

Pa chuckles. "Yes, let's pack up," he says.

We all reel in our lines. Pa carries the old tin bucket full of fish. Lucy and I carry the rods and tackle boxes. We load up our catch and head home.

On the way back, Pa says, "I think you just found a secret weapon for our team! I have to hand it to you, Kylie Jean. You're a fishing queen!"

Fishing Tip #4

Keep blue catfish bait simple! Use fresh bait, cut or whole.

Chapter Five
Fish Camp

On Thursday evening, Pa calls with a special invitation. He wants to take Lucy and me to the family fish camp on Arrowhead Lake for the weekend! He'll pick us up right after school on Friday. I run over to Daddy, who is sitting in the living room.

"Daddy, can I go fishing with Pa and Lucy at the fish camp this weekend?" I ask.

"Of course you can," says Daddy. "T.J. and I might see you there. We're thinking of going to the camp too."

At first, I'm surprised, but there is room for everyone at the camp. I just hope we can get enough practice fishing so we can win the contest!

"We'll see you there then!" I reply.

I run up to my room to pack. Ugly Brother comes too.

"Do you want to help?" I ask him.

He barks, "Ruff, ruff!" Then he drags my special pink duffle bag out of the closet.

"Nothing fancy," I remind him. "It's just the fish camp! Okay?"

"Ruff, ruff!"

Together Ugly Brother and I fill my bag with jeans, sweatshirts, long johns, and thick socks. When my bag is full, I tap it on the side.

"Do you think I have everything I need in here?" I ask.

He barks, "Ruff!"

Uh-oh! One bark means no!

"What did I forget?" I ask.

Ugly Brother nudges his nose into the bag and tries to crawl inside.

"Wait a minute!" I say. "I know you want to come with us, but you have to stay here this time."

Ugly Brother looks a bit sad, but he crawls out of the bag and sits right next to me. "Ruff, ruff," he barks.

I pet the top of his head and give him a big ol' hug. "Don't worry, I'll be back soon," I say.

On Friday after school, Pa picks us up in his truck. He has his gear in the back and a big cooler full of food. On the way, Lucy and I play the alphabet road sign game. We also sing songs, and we talk about school.

We drive and drive until we come to a turnoff marked by a red bandana. We take the long dirt road that twists and turns right to the river's edge. When we finally get to our family fish camp at Arrowhead Lake, another truck is already parked there.

"That's T.J.'s truck!" I shout.

Lucy asks, "What's he doing here?"

Pa replies, "I reckon he's doing what we're doing — getting ready for the contest."

"Yup, Daddy told me they might be here," I say.

We unload the truck and carry everything to the cabin. The camp cabin is a pretty, rustic log building. It's just one big room with a kitchen area on one side and a bathroom on the other. In the middle of the room there is a table and chairs. Around the edges of the room are four cots and two sets of bunk beds.

Lucy points to the cooler. "What did you pack in there?" she asks.

"I packed fresh catfish for a campfire dinner down by the river. For lunches, I packed some jerky, sandwiches, and fruit. For breakfasts, I packed bacon and eggs."

"Sounds delicious," I reply. "Let's get down to the river and do some fishing!"

We see T.J. and Daddy when we get to the river.

Daddy says, "We're all here!"

"Let's just hope there'll be enough fish for all of us!" Pa replies.

* * *

Lucy and I fish day and night, all weekend long, and learn several new things about fishing. Pa teaches Lucy and me all about running trot lines. A trot line is a long cord tied from one side of the river to the other with fish hooks dangling down from it. You can sure catch a lot of fish on those lines. Lucy and I can't believe all the fish! We fish from the dock, and we fish from our boat too. In the evening, Daddy and Pa tell all of us stories by the fire.

Pa says, "Have you ever heard about a big ol' catfish known near and far as Granddaddy Whiskers?"

"Everyone tries to catch Granddaddy Whiskers," says Daddy.

T.J. adds, "No one can, though. A lot of people, including Daddy and Pa, have tried!"

"Every fisherman in the whole county has tried," Pa continues. "But I reckon that fish is just too smart to get caught."

I get a gleam in my eye.

Lucy looks at me. "I bet I know just what you're thinking," she says. "You want to catch Granddaddy Whiskers."

"Yup!" I say.

T.J. doesn't think anyone can catch Granddaddy Whiskers, and that makes me really want to catch that fish! He'll never guess our secret, though. Pa and I keep the cans of Spam we brought with us hidden in his truck.

T.J. says, "I love you, Lil' Bit, but I really want to win. I want to meet Rick Allen."

"I love you too, but I plan to be the big winner!" I tell him.

All the way home on Sunday night, all I can think of is finding Granddaddy Whiskers. We're sure to win the contest, if I can catch that fish! And I will be a Fishing Queen!

Fishing Tip #5

Winter and spring are the best times of year to catch blue cats.

Chapter Six
Finding Granddaddy Whiskers

I have decided that catching Granddaddy Whiskers might be more exciting than being a real true Fishing Queen! I have to find him before I can catch him, so I plan to talk to some experts on Tuesday right after school. Arrowhead Lake is really big, and I need to narrow down the choices for fishing spots.

When I get home that day, I ask Momma if I can ride my bike downtown.

"Can I go to the Coffee Cup Café, please, Momma?" I ask her.

Momma asks, "What do you plan to do at the café?"

"I need to talk to a bunch of fishermen about a big ol' blue cat!" I reply. "If Granddaddy Whiskers does exist, I need to know where he's been spotted."

Momma laughs. "Okay then. Grab your jacket, and Ugly Brother, and I will walk with you. We could use some exercise."

I call Ugly Brother, and he is so excited. He's waggin' his little tail like crazy!

"You are going with me to the café," I tell him. "I'm riding my bike, so you'll have to try to keep up with me!"

He barks, "Ruff, ruff."

I get Ugly Brother's leash. Then the three of us head down Peachtree Lane straight to the town square and the Coffee Cup Café. Before I go in, I tie Ugly Brother's leash to the bike rack.

I say, "Be good, and we'll bring you a treat. Would you like to know what it is?"

He barks, "Ruff, ruff."

I say, "I'll give you a clue. It's your favorite breakfast treat!"

Ugly Brother jumps up and down with excitement. He has figured out my clue. He knows that if he is good, I'm going to bring him some bacon!

Inside the café, the tables all have blue-and-white checked tablecloths and vases with fake sunflowers in them. It looks cheerful in here, even if it's a blustery day outside. The owner, Miss Opal, comes over to seat me.

"Would you like a table by the window so you can watch your doggie?" she asks.

I reply, "No, ma'am. That's very nice of you, but I'd like to sit at the table with those fellas over there. My momma will sit by the window."

I point to Mr. Strick's table. He's one of our neighbors, and he's sitting with Old Man Moore.

Timothy John is there too. Then I remember that Momma says you should never point at people because it's really rude. I put my hands behind my back lickety-split.

Miss Opal looks surprised. She says, "All right then, we'll check with the gentlemen and see if that's okay."

We walk over, and when we get close, I call out, "Hello, Mr. Strick."

He says, "Well, hey there, Kylie Jean."

"Can I sit with y'all and ask you some questions?" I ask.

"Sure thing, little gal," he says. "Hope we know the answers!"

"Thanks," I say as I sit down.

Miss Opal says that I am too young for coffee, so she will bring me some hot chocolate. I tell the table that I am here to listen to fish tales about Granddaddy Whiskers.

Mr. Strick, Old Man Moore, and Timothy John all start talking at once. A mighty gush of words spills out in a loud tangle, and I can't understand any of them! I whistle, loud and long. They stop and look at me.

"This would be easier if you could each take turns telling me about Granddaddy Whiskers," I tell them.

Mr. Strick says, "That Granddaddy Whiskers is a legend. He's been around for a real long time."

"Well, from what Pa says, he is pretty old by now," I say.

Mr. Strick continues, "A normal blue catfish lives about twenty years. But folks swear they've been seeing Granddaddy Whiskers in Arrowhead Lake for nearly seventy-five years, so I'd guess your pa is right about that."

Mr. John says, "Granddaddy Whiskers is not your typical blue cat. Some fish are just legendary! He's been around for so many years, but he's hard to spot. I do think I saw him once near the dock by Easy Street. He was nearly as big as a crocodile!"

Mr. Moore grunts and says, "Oh, yeah, I really did see him over near the old Walton place. It was a clear day, and I saw him swim right up beside my boat! That Granddaddy Whiskers was bigger than an ol' crocodile! My son was with me that day. Just ask him!"

Not to be outdone, Mr. Strick tells the tallest tale so far. "Once when I was fishing down at Broken Line Point, Granddaddy Whiskers came right up to the dock. He swam over, just as pretty as you please. Then something happened that to this day I still can't believe! That ol' fish jumped right up and ate my bait right out of my hand! I guess he was hungry for chicken livers and didn't want to wait for me to bait them on a hook."

Everyone at the table is suddenly quiet.

Finally, I say, "Those were some awesome fish tales! I wanted to find out just where Granddaddy Whiskers has been spotted, and now I know. Before it gets dark, I'm going to have to get on home for dinner. Thanks for the stories!"

"Happy to oblige, Miss Kylie Jean," they say. "And good luck!"

I get up and walk over to Momma's table. I give her a thumbs-up. "Mission accomplished," I say.

Momma smiles. Miss Opal hands me a packet of bacon, and we're out the door. Ugly Brother is overjoyed with his greasy treat!

Fishing Tip #6

Fish with confidence!
If you believe you will catch a fish, you will!

Chapter Seven
Tackle Box Treasure

On Wednesday, with only two more days until the contest, Pa takes me back to the Sports Shack to get a new tackle box! Inside the shop, they have a whole wall stacked floor to ceiling with them. They have big ones and small ones. There are tackle boxes in khaki, red, green, camo, brown, and every shade of blue. I am looking for a special color, though.

Pa asks, "Which one do you like?"

"You know pink is my signature color," I tell him. "I just wish they had a pink one. If they did, it would match my pink fishing vest."

Pa steps over to the counter. He has a chat with Ray. Ray scratches his head, then he smiles from ear to ear and disappears into the back storeroom. He comes back out with a small cardboard box.

"This was a special order," Ray tells me. "But the customer never came in to pick it up. I was about to send it off for a credit, but I think you might like it."

Ray and Pa open the box and pull out a small pink tackle box!

Ray says, "What do you think?"

"I think I love it! It's perfect!" I tell him.

"You heard the little lady," Pa says. "We'll take that tackle box!"

I don't even want to put the tackle box back in the cardboard box. On the way home, I look through all the dividers and spots for hooks and lures. When we get back home, I thank Pa and give him a big squeezy hug!

I have a big project to work on, so I head right into the garage. I want to make a fishing map, but first I take all my fishing tackle out of T.J.'s old box and lay it on Daddy's workbench. Then I carefully sort the various styles and sizes of hooks, weights, pink synthetic worms, crank bait, and jigs.

I have a lot more tackle than I thought I did. I hope it will all fit in my new lucky tackle box!

I start putting everything into the different sections of my new box, starting with the pink worms. They're my favorite! The contest is just a couple of days away now, and I want to be ready!

Just then, T.J. walks into the garage. "Lil' Bit, I've been looking for you. You know I want to win," he tells me. "But I wish we could both win."

"Thanks!" I tell him. "I sure hope one of us wins!"

T.J. has a small box in his pocket. He pulls it out and hands it to me. "I think I picked the perfect day to give you this!" he says. "It's something to add to your tackle box."

I open the box. Inside is a large circle hook. "Thank you, but I already have several circle hooks," I say.

"Not like this one," he tells me. "It's a special lucky hook!"

I look at it closely, but it just seems ordinary to me.

"I caught my very first fish with that hook," T.J. continues. "And even on the worst fishing day, I can always catch something with it! You should use my lucky hook on the day of the contest."

I give T.J. a big squeezy hug! "Now I understand that this lucky hook is a treasure," I tell him. "You're the best brother in the whole wide world. Thanks!"

"You're welcome," he says. "Oh, and you're my favorite sister."

I think about what he just said and realize I'm his only sister! "You're teasing me again, but I forgive you because I have your lucky hook," I say. "It's going to help me win the contest!"

* * *

Later that night, I get my fishing map
started. Using a poster board, I make a giant
map of Arrowhead Lake. I plan to mark all the
Granddaddy Whiskers sightings I've heard about.
Ugly Brother tries to help, but he just keeps sitting
on the map!

"Why don't you sit on the bed and watch me,"
I suggest. "Then you can let me know if I make a
mistake."

Ugly Brother barks, "Ruff, ruff." Then he jumps up on my bed. His head wobbles back and forth, following me as I draw on the map.

"I'm going to draw a circle with a fish in it everywhere someone has spotted Granddaddy Whiskers," I tell him.

He barks again. "Ruff, ruff."

I think about the stories from the café. I mark Easy Street, the old Walton place, and Broken Line Point.

When I'm done, I study the map. "Where do you think we can catch that fish?" I ask.

Ugly Brother jumps down and circles the map three times. Finally, he steps onto the map right at Blackwater Cove.

"Do you think that's where Granddaddy Whiskers is hiding?" I ask.

"Ruff, ruff," he barks. That means yes!

"It would be a mighty good place for Granddaddy Whiskers to give a fisherman the slip," I tell him.

I draw a fish in a circle right on top of Blackwater Cove with a little question mark beside it. It's only two more days until the contest. I sure hope Pa and I can catch that big ol' blue cat.

Fishing Tip #7

If you want to catch catfish,
use a large circle hook or a J-hook.

Chapter Eight
Tie, Cast, Reel

Saturday morning, way before dawn, Daddy, T.J., Pa, and I drive out to Arrowhead Lake. I am dressed warmly and have my pink life jacket, pink tackle box, and my best rod and reel.

It's a short drive to the lake. Pa follows T.J.'s truck, and we arrive at the same time. There are trucks, boats, and boat trailers everywhere you look, plus tons of people ready to fish. They look like ants at a picnic!

Pa parks the truck and goes to the sign-in area to register our team with one of the judges. When he gets back, he says, "Now we'll have to wait in line to use the boat slip."

Daddy and T.J. are waiting for the boat slip too. While we wait, Pa and I go over all the supplies we'll need for the day. That way we can make sure we have it all loaded in the boat and won't forget anything!

Pa asks, "Do we have life jackets, rods and reels, tackle boxes, water, and snacks?"

I reply, "Check, check, check, check, and check!"

Pa laughs.

"Are you ready to win this contest and catch Granddaddy Whiskers?" I ask.

"I sure am!" he replies. "Are you ready for some fishing fun?"

"Yup!" I say. "You know it!"

Before long, we are backing the truck up to the boat ramp. Daddy and T.J. help us get the boat into the water, and Pa ties it to an old dock post. Then I wait in the boat while Pa goes to park his truck. We all help Daddy and T.J. get their boat in the water too.

We still have a lot of time to wait for all the other fishermen and women to get signed in and ready to go. The contest starts at 6 a.m. sharp, so that'll be when all the boats head out and the fishing finally begins!

While I wait for Pa, I go through the supplies one last time. The Spam seems to be missing.

"Oh no!" I yell.

When Pa gets back to the boat, I hop out. "Pa, we left our secret bait in the truck!" I shout.

"It's okay!" he hollers. "We still have time. I'll go back to the truck to get it."

I sigh with relief. Before you know it, Pa is back, dropping the brown paper sack with the Spam into the boat.

"I have a plan," I say. "According to my map, we need to head over to Blackwater Cove."

"Does your map tell you that's the spot where we can catch Granddaddy Whiskers?" Pa asks.

"Yes, sir, it does!" I reply. "I think that's the best place to start."

"Sounds like a good plan to me!" says Pa. "We can fish along the way too."

Finally, it's time for the contest to start, and we glide out onto the water. Once we find our perfect spot, I give my new lucky hook from T.J. a little pat and cast out into the water.

Soon Pa and I catch some nice-sized blue cats, but we'll have to catch a really big one to win this contest. We have to have the catch that weighs the most. The day seems to be going pretty well.

"We're doing great!" I say.

Pa says, "Don't jinx us!"

Suddenly Pa gets a bite. He thinks it's a big fish, because it's fighting pretty hard. He works and works to reel it in. I watch excitedly, waiting to see the size of the cat.

Instead, I cry, "Oh no! Poor little guy! Pa, it's a snapping turtle."

"See, we're jinxed," he says. "I need to get the hook out of this poor guy."

It's a small turtle, so Pa holds him by his sides and uses his pliers to get the hook out. Then he gently drops him back overboard.

Getting that turtle free from the hook has taken up valuable fishing time, but we're pretty close to Blackwater Cove now. I am so excited that I cast out, getting a little ahead of myself. We're not even all the way into the cove yet!

I wait to see if I get a nibble. Pa is casting from the other side of the boat, and he catches something. I secure my rod and help him bring in a nice-sized blue cat.

"That fish is a beauty!" I cry. "I bet it weighs fifty pounds. Way to go, Pa!"

Pa says, "I can see that blue cats would love this deep, dark water. We should head deeper into the cove and see if old Granddaddy Whiskers shows up."

"Great plan!" I reply. I try to reel in my line, but it's stuck!

"Let me try," says Pa.

But he can't get the line in either. Shaking his head, he says, "Unfortunately, with the lair of the mighty fish straight ahead, your line is snagged!"

"What do you think it's caught on?" I ask.

"No telling," Pa says. "We'll have to get closer."

He steers us into the shallow water closer to shore. I scan the water, looking to see where my fishing line will lead me.

Then I shout, "I caught a stump!"

"It's okay," says Pa. "You caught a stump, and I caught a turtle!"

We aim the boat as close as we can to the stump. Pa pulls on his high boots, puts the pliers in his pocket, and wades into the shallow water.

"Watch out for gators!" I call.

"I think I better watch out for snakes instead," he says. "No one's ever seen a gator out here."

The water in Blackwater Cove is so dark and deep, we might not even see a snake coming. The sunlight glistens on the surface, but everything below is hidden.

"Be careful, Pa," I tell him.

Pa says, "Don't worry, I will."

Finally, Pa reaches out and snips the hook, leaving my line sinking down into the water.

He wades back to the boat and climbs in. Giving the motor a quick crank, Pa starts it up again. He steers us into a spot near the far side of the cove.

"Thanks for untangling me," I say.

"You're welcome," Pa replies. "Now, if you think that old fish is nearby, maybe we should give that Spam a try."

"I'd bet my allowance he's here!" I say.

Pa and I both put Spam on our hooks and dangle the tantalizing treats into the water. Then we wait quietly to see if the legendary fish will ever come.

"I heard ol' Granddaddy Whiskers likes chicken livers," Pa says. "Maybe we should have brought some just in case."

"I don't think so," I reply.

"What makes you so sure?" he asks.

"I just have a hunch he might like something different," I tell him. "Lots of folks try to catch him with livers because they've heard the story about him jumping out of the water to eat them."

Pa says, "True."

We wait and wait for hours. Good fishermen must be patient.

I watch the shore. I see birds, a snake, and squirrels going about their daily routine. I'm glad the snake didn't get close to Pa. It's too far away to tell if it's a venomous snake. I like watching the shifting clouds in the brilliant blue sky. As they move, they make a castle, a pirate, a butterfly, and a train.

"Pa, can I tell you a story?" I ask.

"Do you know one?" he asks.

"I just made one up and it goes like this . . . once upon a time, there was a squirrel princess," I tell him.

"Wait, I've never heard of a squirrel princess before," Pa says.

"Of course not, I just made it up with my imagination," I say. "The squirrel princess lived in a wonderful castle in a tree with all of her loyal subjects."

"I see," says Pa.

"Her father, the squirrel king, wanted her to marry a mean old prince, but she thought that would be so boring! You see, she dreamed of being a pirate, not a princess. One day she woke up and decided to take the train all the way to the ocean. She was sure she would find a pirate ship there."

Pa sighs. "Is that the end of the story?" he asks. "What happens? Does she get to be a pirate?"

"No, it's not the end," I reply. "I don't know what happens next, because I haven't made up the rest yet."

"Okay," says Pa.

Then I ask, "Pa, do you think maybe Granddaddy Whiskers is just a story?"

"If you don't believe in him, you'll never catch him," he replies.

"I do believe in him," I say. "Really, I do. It's just that we've been out here a long, long time."

Pa thinks for a minute. "All good things take time," he says. "A good fisherman knows how to fill quiet time. No one should get bored fishing! And this is a really smart fish. If you want to reel him in, you'll have to be patient."

Fishing Tip #8

Change your fishing line often, because old line breaks easily.

Chapter Nine
Big Cat Blues

In spite of the sun shining down, Pa and I feel a chill in our bones. It is getting late in the day, and I think Pa is right. That ol' fish is just too smart for us!

We are both getting tired, and the contest is almost over. But suddenly, my bobber sinks deep, and I feel the serious pull on my line of something *really* big.

"Pa, this is it! I think it's Granddaddy Whiskers!" I shout.

Pa leans to my side of the boat. The fish is nearly pulling me over the edge. "Hold on tight!" he shouts.

He grabs onto my rod, and we both wrestle the fish. The boat rolls back and forth with our movements.

"It's a big one!" Pa yells.

"I can see the fish!" I shout. "He's a big, dark blue — almost black — catfish with a white belly. Do you think it's him?"

Pa says, "Let's see if it is . . ."

Excitedly, we net the gigantic fish and pull him over the side of boat. Pa looks at him lying across the bottom of the boat and examines him from tip to tail.

"What do you think?" I ask him. "Is it Granddaddy Whiskers?"

"Yup," Pa replies. Slowly he begins to grin. "I reckon that's him. He must weigh nearly a hundred pounds!"

"Yippee!" I yell.

"We did it!" Pa shouts. "We caught him. It's Granddaddy Whiskers!"

"Hooray!" I yell. "We got the biggest fish of all, Granddaddy Whiskers!"

Suddenly, Pa looks a little sad.

"What's wrong, Pa?" I ask.

"You know, the secret of a great fisherman is realizing that some fish deserve to be thrown back," he says. "We could probably win the contest with Granddaddy Whiskers, but this legendary fish has outwitted fishermen since I was a boy. If you believe such fish tales, that is. Truth be told, he's probably the great-grandson of the first Granddaddy Whiskers."

I can understand plain as day that Pa wants to release Granddaddy Whiskers. I look at that big ol' fish lying there in the boat. He is majestic. His inky black body is covered with water droplets that look like diamonds in the sunlight. I look straight into his eyes. It's almost like he's waiting for me to say something.

"Granddaddy Whiskers," I say, "I think you let me catch you because you knew I wanted to so much. Anyway, that was before I met you. You don't know me, but I am the queen of many things, and I have just figured out that you are the real true king of this lake. You and I are going to be forever friends, Granddaddy Whiskers."

"Well, that was awful nice of you," says Pa.

"Pa, quick, help me get him back in the water!"
I shout.

We carefully ease Granddaddy Whiskers up
and over the edge of the boat. Then, with a huge
splash, the legendary blue cat slips deep into the
water.

I look out across the lake, hoping to see him one more time. Pa is looking too. But Granddaddy Whiskers is gone.

Pa says, "Only a real true fishing queen would lose a fishing contest to save such a noble fish!"

"I think we'd better keep our big catch a secret," I say. "Otherwise everyone will be out here trying to catch him."

"Good idea," replies Pa. "I won't tell a soul."

We head back to shore. I know I should be sad because I'm not going to win the contest, but I am so happy about meeting Granddaddy Whiskers that I don't even care.

* * *

Back at the dock, the other fishing teams are weighing their fish. I look for Daddy and T.J. Without Granddaddy Whiskers, I don't think we'll win, but I sure hope Daddy and T.J. have some really big fish. Maybe the Carters will win today after all.

I see them and wave. I run to the end of the dock where their boat is tied.

T.J. brags, "We have one fish that might just weigh seventy-five pounds! I think I'll be meeting Rick Allen in person!"

Daddy asks, "How did y'all do?"

Pa says, "We didn't catch any really big ones. We had some bad luck in the morning, and it slowed us down."

Just then, a contest judge makes an announcement. "Attention! All weigh-ins are complete. We have determined the Winter Catfish Classic Team Fishing Contest's winning team. Remember, the winning team wins a brand new fishing boat, and they will meet Rick Allen!"

My heart is pounding. I so want Daddy and T.J. to win!

"This year's winning team is Mr. Carter and his son, T.J.!" the judge says.

Daddy and T.J. look surprised and happy. We all give each other big ol' hugs.

"I'm so proud of you!" I tell them.

After he and Daddy accept their prize, they walk back over. "I know you didn't win, Lil' Bit, but did you see Granddaddy Whiskers?" he asks.

I reply, "You won't believe me, but we really did! We tried to catch him, but he got away."

Daddy laughs. "Sounds like you've got the big cat blues!" he says.

I wink at Pa, and he winks back. Deep inside, I know I'm a Fishing Queen!

"You never know," I say. "Granddaddy Whiskers is still out there . . . maybe I'll catch him tomorrow in our brand new boat!"

Fishing Tip #9

Be safe while fishing!

Always have an adult with you when you're near water.

Also, always wear a life vest.

Marci Bales Peschke was born in Indiana, grew up in Florida, and now lives in Texas with her husband, two children, and a feisty cat named Cookie. She loves reading and watching movies.

When **Tuesday Mourning** was a little girl, she knew she wanted to be an artist when she grew up. Now, she is an illustrator who lives in Utah. She especially loves illustrating books for kids and teenagers. When she isn't illustrating, Tuesday loves spending time with her husband, who is an actor, and their two sons and one daughter.

Glossary

bait (BAYT)—a small amount of food put on a hook to attract a fish

bandana (ban-DAN-uh)—a large, brightly colored square of fabric

bobber (BAH-bur)—a small ball attached to a fishing line that floats on water

expert (EK-spurt)—someone who has a special skill or knows a lot about a subject

research (REE-surch)—information about a subject that one finds through reading, investigating, or experimenting

Spam (SPAM)—a type of canned meat

synthetic (sin-THET-ik)—made by humans rather than found in nature

Talk!

1. Kylie Jean surprises her mom by asking Pa to be on her fishing team. Do you like surprises? Have you ever had fun surprising someone? Has anyone given you a good surprise?

2. Kylie Jean and Lucy research catfish at the library. What is your favorite thing to do at the library? Ask an adult to show you some fun things to do at the library!

3. Kylie Jean and Pa must be patient while they fish. When do you practice patience? What fun things can you think of to do the next time you must wait? Talk about it!

Be Creative!

1. Pa told Kylie Jean the exciting story about Granddaddy Whiskers. Imagine your own tall tale. Tell your story to a friend!

2. If Granddaddy Whiskers could talk, what do you think he would say to Kylie Jean before she put him back in the water? What do you think he would say after Kylie Jean let him go? Use a silly fish voice to act out the scene. Don't forget the whiskers!

3. Mr. Carter and T.J. won a boat at the fishing contest. If you could design a boat, what would it look like? Draw a picture and show it to a friend!

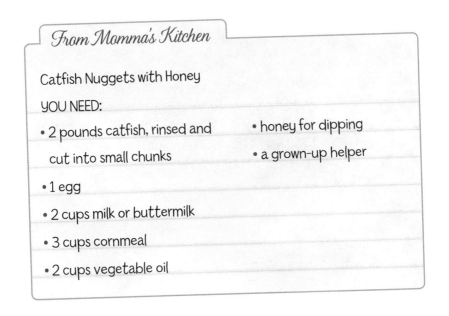

This is the perfect treat for any Fishing Queen!
Just make sure to ask a grown-up for help.

Love, Kylie Jean

From Momma's Kitchen

Catfish Nuggets with Honey

YOU NEED:

- 2 pounds catfish, rinsed and cut into small chunks
- 1 egg
- 2 cups milk or buttermilk
- 3 cups cornmeal
- 2 cups vegetable oil
- honey for dipping
- a grown-up helper

1. Pour oil into large skillet and place on medium-high heat.

2. In small bowl, beat egg. Add the milk and beat again.

3. Put the cornmeal in a large bowl.

4. Dip each nugget into the egg and milk mixture.

5. Roll each nugget in the cornmeal until coated.

6. Ask an adult to place the coated nuggets in the oil. Fry for 3 minutes, or until golden brown and flaky.

7. Let cool for 5 to 10 minutes. Serve with honey for dipping.

Yum, yum!

THE FUN DOESN'T STOP HERE!

Discover more at www.capstonekids.com

💜 Videos & Contests
✿ Games & Puzzles
💜 Friends & Favorites
✿ Authors & Illustrators

Find cool websites and more books like this one at www.facthound.com. Just type in the Book ID: **9781479599004** and you're ready to go!

3 1333 04641 9535